Restricted Circulation

NAOMI LAZARD

What Amanda Saw

illustrated by
PAUL O. ZELINSKY

GREENWILLOW BOOKS
New York

10   9   8   7   6   5   4   3   2   1

Library of Congress Cataloging in Publication Data
Lazard, Naomi.   What Amanda Saw.
Summary: Amanda's cat attends a special celebration
on the last night of summer vacation.
[1. Parties—Fiction. 2 Animals—Fiction]
I. Zelinsky, Paul O. II. Title PZ7.L447Wh   [E]   80-14516
ISBN 0-688-80272-9   ISBN 0-688-84272-0 (lib. bdg.)

FOR VIRGINIA
–N.L.

FOR DUSTY
–P.O.Z.

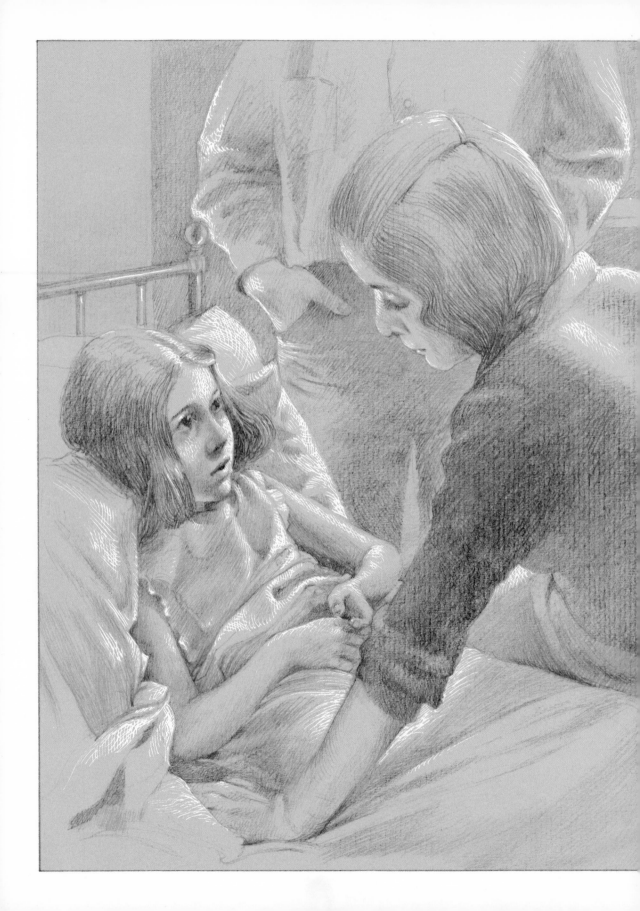

It was the end of summer. Evenings were getting cooler. The sun wasn't the red-hot ball of fire it had been, and in the late afternoons it hung low and long in the sky. And when night came, it came fast.

The family was getting ready to leave the summer cottage. All that evening, after dinner, they made their last-minute preparations. Amanda called her friends again to say good-bye.

Finally it was time to go to bed. It was very late, almost eleven o'clock, far past Amanda's usual bedtime. She went to her bedroom and got into bed. Her mother and father kissed her good night.

"Tomorrow is the big day," Amanda's mother said, "so go to sleep immediately."

"Yes, that's right," Amanda's father said.

"But where is Bubble?" Amanda asked. Bubble was her cat and he always slept with Amanda, curling up at the foot of her bed.

"Where is that cat?" Amanda's mother asked of nobody in particular.

Late as it was, Amanda got out of bed and went downstairs. The three of them looked all over the house and even opened the doors to call Bubble home. But he wasn't anywhere in the house and he didn't come to their calls.

"We can't leave without Bubble," Amanda said.

"Of course not," Amanda's mother said. "Don't worry. He'll come home soon."

Amanda couldn't get to sleep. She was worried about Bubble. It's true that *sometimes* he spent the night away from home and didn't come back until the next day, but this night was special. It was the last night and they wouldn't be coming back for almost a year.

Amanda had to find Bubble. After a while she got out of bed and went, very quietly, downstairs. She opened the door and went outside into the moonlight. She started calling very softly, "Bubble! Bubble! Bubble, come home!"

But Bubble didn't answer her call.

Amanda went farther and farther from the house, down the path and through a grove of trees. She passed the brook and went even farther into a field. Every once in a while she called, "Bubble! Bubble!"

At last Amanda came to a fence. Beyond it the land belonged to one of their neighbors, a farmer. He had built the fence to keep his animals from straying. It was made of slats of wood. Amanda looked between the slats and saw an extraordinary sight. A long table had been set up, and around the table, each one wearing a festive hat, were the animals who lived in the countryside. Bubble was there too, sitting at the head of the table. Amanda stood there without moving and watched and listened.

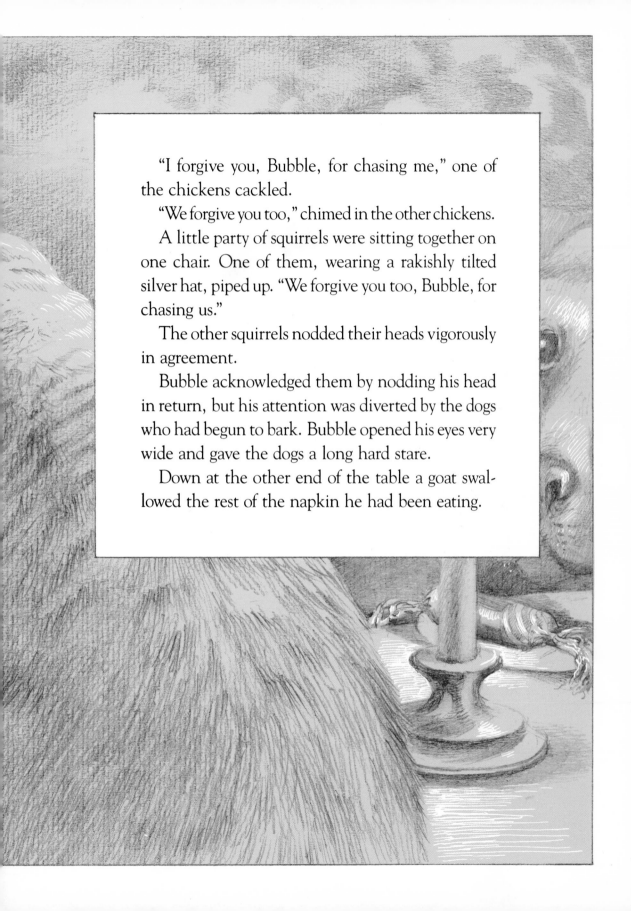

"I forgive you, Bubble, for chasing me," one of
the chickens cackled.

"We forgive you too," chimed in the other chickens.

A little party of squirrels were sitting together on
one chair. One of them, wearing a rakishly tilted
silver hat, piped up. "We forgive you too, Bubble, for
chasing us."

The other squirrels nodded their heads vigorously
in agreement.

Bubble acknowledged them by nodding his head
in return, but his attention was diverted by the dogs
who had begun to bark. Bubble opened his eyes very
wide and gave the dogs a long hard stare.

Down at the other end of the table a goat swal-
lowed the rest of the napkin he had been eating.

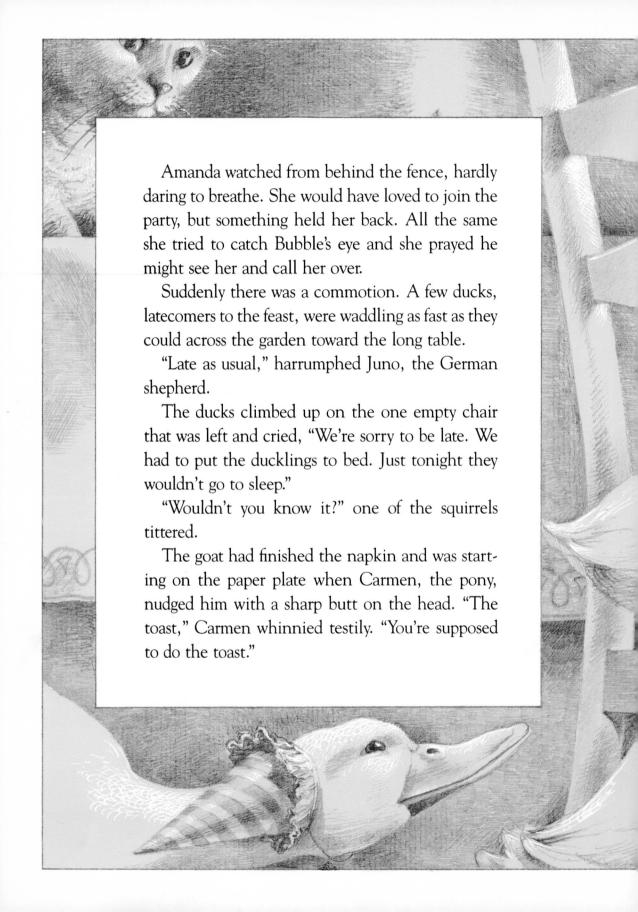

Amanda watched from behind the fence, hardly daring to breathe. She would have loved to join the party, but something held her back. All the same she tried to catch Bubble's eye and she prayed he might see her and call her over.

Suddenly there was a commotion. A few ducks, latecomers to the feast, were waddling as fast as they could across the garden toward the long table.

"Late as usual," harrumphed Juno, the German shepherd.

The ducks climbed up on the one empty chair that was left and cried, "We're sorry to be late. We had to put the ducklings to bed. Just tonight they wouldn't go to sleep."

"Wouldn't you know it?" one of the squirrels tittered.

The goat had finished the napkin and was starting on the paper plate when Carmen, the pony, nudged him with a sharp butt on the head. "The toast," Carmen whinnied testily. "You're supposed to do the toast."

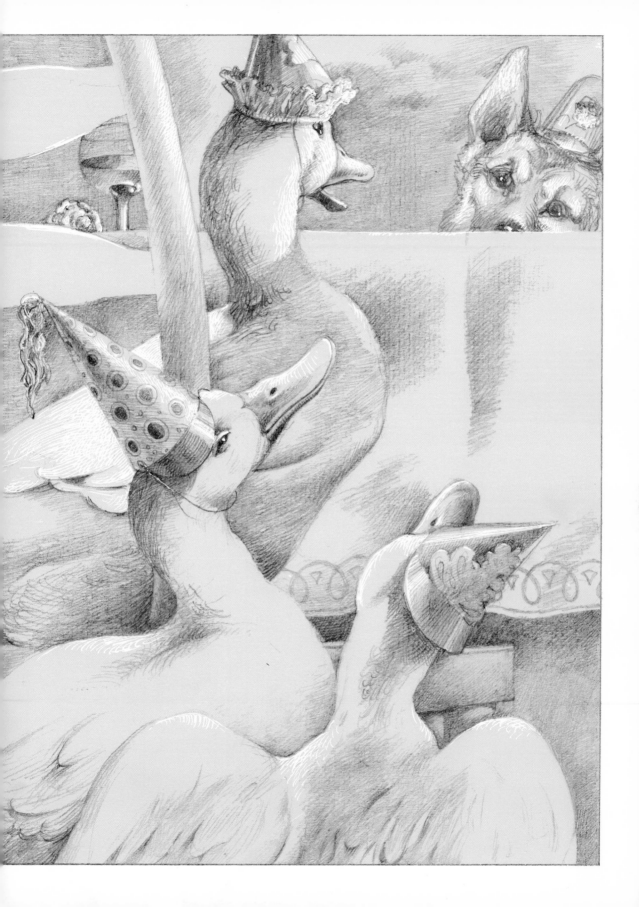

The goat looked up with an embarrassed expression. "Is it time?"

"You've been so busy you haven't noticed. Look over there." Carmen pointed her long nose toward the shed.

The goat glanced around. In fact a sheep was coming along the path carrying a large cake on a round tin tray.

"It most certainly *is* time," the pony brayed loudly.

The goat (Amanda never did catch his name) rose with dignity. This was difficult because some pieces of the paper plate he had been eating were sticking out of his mouth. Carmen wiped them away.

The goat bleated a soft "Thanks" and then addressed the company at large, "Silence. A little silence, please."

The other animals, except for the pony of course, kept chattering to each other in a lively way. On the fringes of the group, just out of reach, several birds who had not, it appeared, been invited to the party, flew back and forth among themselves. The sounds they made as they twittered and cheeped and sang were a continual accompaniment to the noise of the animals.

"Silence!" the goat bleated in the highest register of his voice.

"I'll second that," one of the chickens clucked.

"Make way for the cake," the sheep baa-ed. Amanda thought he looked terribly important.

"Oh, the cake," the squirrels chittered.

"Silence!" the goat commanded.

Everyone fell silent. Even the birds folded their wings and were still.

In the hush Bubble could be heard. "Let the birds come too." He had a majestic air.

The birds did not need another invitation. They flew briskly to the table and began eating whatever crumbs there were. Amanda almost clapped her hands, she was so delighted.

The birds ate, as was their custom, very quickly. They hopped around among the scattered plates and bits of leftover food on the table and soon they too were still.

"Now," the goat assumed his most important tone, "I want to propose a toast to Bubble."

"A toast to Bubble," echoed the chickens.

"A toast to our Bubble!" yelped a mongrel dog whose name, Amanda knew, was Whipper.

At that very moment the sheep presented Bubble with the cake he had been carrying. It was, Amanda noticed, a fine large cake with many layers in the shape of a sawed-off pyramid. It was

decorated with the grass that Bubble liked to chew. The sheep placed the cake on its tin tray squarely in front of Bubble.

"What's the toast?" the ducks quacked out.

"The toast is," the goat answered, "that I say there isn't another cat like Bubble. Here's to Bubble."

"Here's to Bubble!" everyone joined in.

All the animals held their goblets high.

"Hurray for Bubble! Hurray! Hurray! Hurray!"

Bubble was grooming himself modestly. But he found time to reach out and lick off a few pieces of grass.

"Speech! Speech!" yapped out the mongrel.

"Speech! We want a speech!" cackled the chickens.

Bubble rose slowly, a little shakily Amanda thought, and for a moment sat on his haunches very quietly. He was watching the birds. They had started twittering again, but soon they stopped. Bubble's eyes could be very commanding, as Amanda knew.

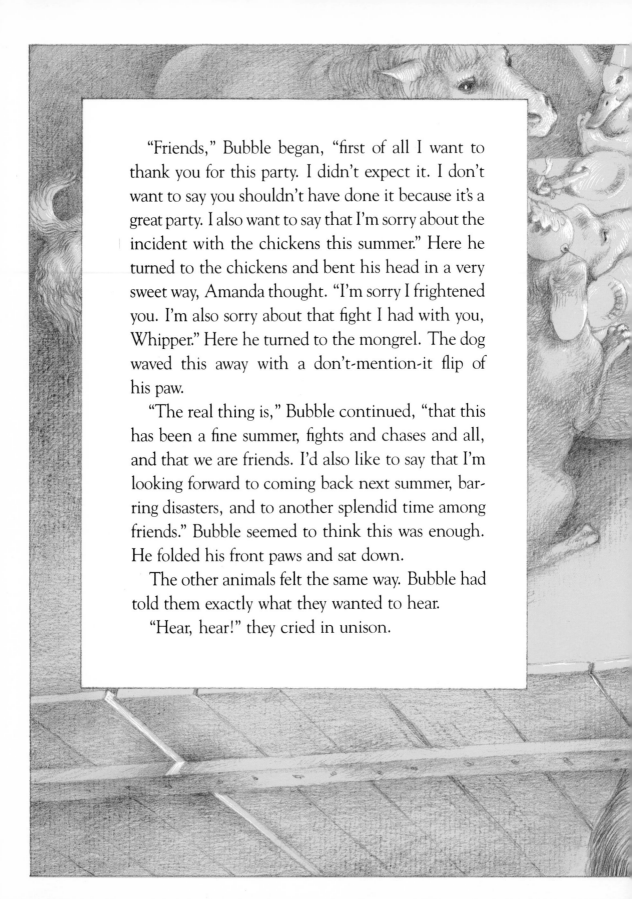

"Friends," Bubble began, "first of all I want to thank you for this party. I didn't expect it. I don't want to say you shouldn't have done it because it's a great party. I also want to say that I'm sorry about the incident with the chickens this summer." Here he turned to the chickens and bent his head in a very sweet way, Amanda thought. "I'm sorry I frightened you. I'm also sorry about that fight I had with you, Whipper." Here he turned to the mongrel. The dog waved this away with a don't-mention-it flip of his paw.

"The real thing is," Bubble continued, "that this has been a fine summer, fights and chases and all, and that we are friends. I'd also like to say that I'm looking forward to coming back next summer, barring disasters, and to another splendid time among friends." Bubble seemed to think this was enough. He folded his front paws and sat down.

The other animals felt the same way. Bubble had told them exactly what they wanted to hear.

"Hear, hear!" they cried in unison.

Then they fell on the cake and very quickly it was all eaten. Bubble got the grass in addition to his portion. The birds got the crumbs.

As soon as the cake was gone and nothing was left but the tin tray it had rested on (now Amanda could see it was actually the lid of a trash can), one of the birds approached Bubble. He had something small in his beak. Amanda could hardly hear what he cheeped as he dropped the thing in his beak. She pressed her head more closely against the fence.

"This is our gift to you, Bubble. Wear it and be well."

That's what Amanda heard the bird twitter.

Bubble sniffed the small object on the table. Amanda strained to see what it was. At last she understood. The bird's gift to Bubble was a bell. It was attached to a fine collar that only birds know how to braid, an almost invisible collar scarcely more than a thread. Bubble pushed the bell with his nose and it made a good sharp ring.

All the animals were waiting for Bubble's response.

After a thoughtful pause Bubble decided. "I'll wear it. And I thank you." In Amanda's opinion that was very gracious of him.

Another round of cheers went up.

Amanda was feeling very sleepy. She tiptoed away from the fence and walked back to the cottage. She opened the door quietly and went up the stairs and into her room. She got into bed without making a sound. She wasn't worried about Bubble anymore so she fell asleep.

When she woke up in the morning, Bubble was there, stretched out at the foot of her bed, sleeping the well-earned sleep of an exhausted but contented cat.

But when Amanda got out of bed, Bubble opened his eyes, arched himself and rippled, and yawned so that every one of his clever white teeth showed.

"Did you have a good time last night, Bubble?" Amanda asked.

Bubble gave her a piercing look, as he sometimes did, as if he had never seen her in his life until that moment.

Just before they left to drive to the city, Bubble drank some milk and ate what was left of his fish. Then he jumped into the back seat of the car beside Amanda, curled up and promptly went to sleep. He slept all the way home.